BABE
PIG IN THE CITY
A Storybook

by Justine Korman and Ron Fontes

Based on the motion picture screenplay written by
George Miller   Judy Morris   Mark Lamprell

Based on characters created by Dick King-Smith

Random House New York

www.randomhouse.com/kids
www.universalstudios.com
Library of Congress Catalog Card Number: 98-066576

ISBN: 0-679-89154-4

Printed in the United States of America 10 9 8 7 6 5 4 3 2 1

Once, dear ones, there lived a little pig with a very big heart. The pig was called Babe, and his human was a quiet farmer named Arthur Hoggett. Against all odds, this unlikely pair of friends won the National Sheepdog Trials.

Babe was famous! Invitations came from all over to open fairs, to demonstrate sheepherding—even to meet the Queen. The fuss was enough to make even the most humble creature giddy. And so it was with our small pink friend.

Farmer Hoggett was eager to return to the simple pleasures of honest work. Just a few days after their homecoming parade, the quiet man was repairing the farm's water pump.

Babe, still dizzy with fame, somehow got it in his head that he could help. But fate turns in a moment. And all it took to change everything was for Babe to lean over to get a better view as Hoggett lowered the new pump down the deep well.

"Boss! *Boss!*" Babe cried. "BOSS!"

All the animals and humans of Hoggett Hollow were soon gathered around the farmer's sickbed. Mrs. Hoggett glared as the guilty pig made his way to her Arthur's side.

Babe's throat choked with remorse. If ever there was a moment in his short life when he wished his words could be understood by humans, this was it.

Babe whispered, "S-s-sorry...Boss."

Life on Hoggett Farm took a turn for the worse. Even *before* her Arthur's calamity, Mrs. Hoggett had been endlessly busy. Now the farmer's wife was overwhelmed with nursing her husband, working the farm, and trying to pay the bills.

One day, Mrs. Hoggett looked up from yet another chore to see two men in suits. By their pale faces and soulless eyes, she knew the men could only have come from one place: the bank!

Mrs. Hoggett panicked. She ran back to the farmhouse as fast as her legs would carry her. There she found a letter inviting Babe to a state fair. All they had to do was show up, and they'd be paid a generous fee! *That* would keep the bank at bay until her Arthur was on his feet again.

Babe tried hard to keep up his courage during the plane trip to the city. He softly sang his favorite tune, "La, la, la. La, la, la…" But the roar of the engines drowned him out.

After they landed, Babe found himself in a big room full of suitcases. He and Mrs. Hoggett were supposed to catch a connecting flight. But a nosy dog in airport security started barking at Babe. The next thing he knew, the boss's wife was being taken away by customs officers. Mrs. Hoggett was questioned, searched, and finally released. But not before she and Babe had missed their flight.

They were stranded!

Mrs. Hoggett soon discovered that hotels did not welcome pigs. "It's only a *little* pig," she told one desk clerk. "Well, it's more of a dog, really," she told another. "He's practically human!" she desperately explained to the next.

Nor could they stay at the airport. "Move on, lady. This isn't a farm," a security guard told them.

They had nowhere to go! But then the night cleaner came over and handed Mrs. Hoggett a little piece of paper with an address:

The Flealands Hotel
349 Random Canal

She looked up at the night cleaner's pink, round face. He looked back at her with tiny, twinkly eyes—just like Babe's!

Babe and Mrs. Hoggett made their way through the bustling metropolis. Finally, after traveling through a maze of back streets and bridges, they found the Flealands Hotel. Mrs. Hoggett knocked on the door.

"I need a room for myself and the wee pig," she said when the landlady answered.

"Are you crazy?" the landlady shrieked. "Animals in *here?* What makes you think we take animals? Am I aware of the city codes and regulations? Yes! Do I support these laws? Certainly! I am a very lawful person." She slammed the door shut.

Mrs. Hoggett did not know where to go. She walked uncertainly around the corner, then heard a *"Pssst!"* The landlady was signaling to her from a dark alley. "How long do you want to stay?" she whispered.

"Two days," Mrs. Hoggett replied.

"Will an attic room do?" the landlady asked.

Mrs. Hoggett was confused. "But you said…"

"That was just for the neighbors, heartless meanies," the landlady explained. "Where do they expect these poor creatures to go?"

The landlady led Mrs. Hoggett and Babe inside her hotel and up the stairs. On the second landing, a little dog zipped out of a doorway and started sniffing Babe all over. The little dog's name was Flealick, and his crippled back legs were mounted on wheels.

The city dog had never seen a creature like Babe before.

"Canine…" Flealick guessed. Then he sniffed again. "Feline. Oh, no, you're a cat!"

"Do I *look* like a cat?" Babe asked.

Flealick's eyes were almost as bad as his nose. "Not sure," he said. "But if you're a cat, you've got no business on this floor!"

After they got to their room, Mrs. Hoggett went back down to the street to call her husband. While she was gone, a tiny monkey named Tug crept into the room and scampered off with her suitcase!

"Hey! That belongs to the boss's wife!" Babe cried. He chased the monkey down the steps to a room on the first floor. There he found a family of chimpanzees living like humans! Babe politely asked for the suitcase. But the chimps—Bob; his brother, Easy; and Bob's pregnant wife, Zootie—were not impressed.

"I may be small, but I can be ferocious," Babe warned.

The chimps backed off, but only because of the arrival of a bigger ape, dressed in a butler's uniform: Thelonius, the orangutan!

Thelonius was even less impressed with Babe. "This lowly, handless, deeply unattractive mud-lover is a pig," he declared.

Their conversation was interrupted by the arrival of Uncle Fugly, the old clown who owned the apes.

At that moment, Mrs. Hoggett returned to discover both her suitcase *and* her pig gone! The landlady begged Mrs. Hoggett not to call the police, who would surely close down her hotel when they discovered all the animals.

Uncle Fugly heard the commotion and quickly hid the pig in a trunk. "But that…that's my human!" Babe protested.

"Shh!" Thelonius hissed.

"I don't care about the clothes," Mrs. Hoggett said. "But the pig—I can't go home without my Arthur's pig!"

Uncle Fugly pretended he'd seen the pig leave the hotel and head toward the beach.

   As Mrs. Hoggett searched for Babe, she accidentally insulted a pair of motorcycle cops with her cries of "Pig, pig, pig!" The cops took off after her and crashed into a guy who was trying to take her purse! In the pileup that followed, two men gluing up a giant poster were knocked off their ladders. Their bucket of glue fell on Mrs. Hoggett's head! The farmer's wife soon found herself purseless, arrested, and very, very sticky.

   Meanwhile, Babe was making his stage debut! Uncle Fugly had stolen the pig so he could use him in his vaudeville act. The innocent pig had agreed to perform in exchange for a big reward. Babe hoped that whatever the reward was, it would help save the farm.

   But after the show, Babe didn't get a reward. In fact, he didn't even get dinner! Uncle Fugly kept all the food for himself.

   Thelonius, who loved Uncle Fugly very much, defended him to the hungry chimps. "You mindless knuckle-walkers! You don't deserve his kindness! He put the very clothes on our backs. He taught us to walk upright. He freed our hands for higher work!"

"But he didn't give me my reward!" protested Babe.

Thelonius threw Babe out the window. *SPLASH!* The pig landed in the canal. "Who's next?" Thelonius asked the cowering chimps.

Babe dragged himself out of the canal and back to the hotel. "There is no reward, is there?" he asked Zootie.

"Oh, little pink thingy," Zootie replied. "This is the city."

The next morning, Uncle Fugly got sick and was carried off to the hospital. Thelonius was devastated. Babe was lonely, scared, and hungry. The farm and the beloved man of few words were starting to seem more and more like a dream.

The long day passed, and no humans returned to the Flealands Hotel. Babe's belly moaned, *"Food, foooood, oh, food!"*

Finally, Bob decided to take action.

Babe followed the chimps outside. "I'll do anything. I *have* to eat!" he cried.

"You don't even have hands," Easy said. "What can you do?"

"I can herd sheep," Babe said.

That gave Bob an idea. He led Babe to the back of a convenience store and pulled open a small hole in the fence. "There are sheep in there," he said.

"Where do you want me to herd them?" Babe asked as he squeezed through the hole.

"Just keep them occupied till we get the necessaries," Bob replied craftily.

"Hello?" Babe called. "Anybody home?"

A huge Doberman lurched out of the shadows and snarled at the pig.

"I'm looking for some sheep," Babe explained.

An even more menacing growl rumbled in the shadows. Suddenly, a bull terrier came charging straight at Babe! The pig turned and ran.

SNAP! The dog's heavy chain stopped him just as the pig wriggled out through the fence.

"Where are your manners?" Babe asked. "I was just trying to have a civil conversation—"

The bull terrier lunged at Babe again. This time he pulled the stake holding his chain right out of the ground!

Babe ran as fast as his little trotters would take him. He turned a corner and found himself in Cardboard City, an alley piled high with boxes that sheltered a community of homeless animals.

Babe tried everything to lose the dogs. But the cruel canines were on his tail!

Babe ran into a garden, the bull terrier close on his heels. The dog's chain hooked on to a lawnmower, but even that didn't slow him down!

Babe ran past a gazebo. The bull terrier came crashing toward him, dragging the lawnmower.

All Babe could do was keep running. Finally, he was too tired to go on. He stopped and looked into the eyes of his pursuer and wondered…Why?

The animals from Cardboard City watched as the bull terrier
lunged toward Babe's collar. It seemed that the pig was doomed!
Then, suddenly, Babe's leather collar broke. He fell into the canal!

The bull terrier jumped in after him. But the lawnmower at the end of his chain got tangled around a newspaper vending machine.

The bull terrier found himself dangling upside down. His head hung just inches above the water. The bull terrier swiped savagely at his own reflection, and the chain slipped. Now his head was under the water!

Babe pulled himself onto the bank and shook himself dry. He was alive!
He was free!

Then he looked back at the bull terrier. Bubbles churned beneath
the dark water. The dog was drowning!

The homeless animals turned away. But Babe could not. He jumped
back into the canal and swam to a small boat. Trotters frantically slap-
ping at the water, the little pig managed to push the boat toward the bull
terrier.

Babe shoved the boat under the dog's body. Coughing and sputtering, the bull terrier managed to pull himself up out of the water. He was alive, but still tangled in the chain.

"Please! Someone, give us a hand!" Babe called.

Little Tug jumped down and unclipped the dog's chain from his collar. Babe swam back to dry land, huffing and puffing.

Suddenly, the tired pig was surrounded by forlorn animals. A bedraggled pink poodle said, "Kind sir, can you help me?"

"Um, where is your human?" Babe asked.

"They belong to someone else now. Someone younger and prettier," the poodle said sadly.

"I—I—I never even h-h-had a hu-hu-human," barked a mangy dog who could not stop scratching.

A starving kitten squeaked weakly, "I'm hungry."

Babe did not know what to do. "Well, it's nice and warm inside the hotel," he began.

Bob stepped forward. "That's not a good idea," he said.

Then an old dog noticed the jar of jellybeans, stolen from the convenience store, that the chimp carried.

"Could that be food?" he asked.

Bob clutched the jar to his chest.

"Have mercy. I'm fainting from hunger," the poodle pleaded.

A hundred voices begged Babe for food.

"Perhaps if we all went inside and lined up? I'm sure there'll be enough to go around," Babe suggested.

"Hey, you're talking as if you're in charge around here," Bob challenged.

A low growl silenced the crowd. A gruff voice said, "I'd say he is." The bull terrier stepped forward. "Whatever the pig says…goes."

All the animals quickly agreed, including Bob.

While the other animals started filing into the hotel, the bull terrier asked Babe if he would wear his spiked collar.

"Um, you're very kind, but that's not necessary," Babe said.

"Pig," said the bull terrier, "if you were to wear my collar, it would honor me."

Babe put on the collar. Together he and the bull terrier went inside to oversee the sharing of the jellybeans.

But a few jellybeans apiece were not enough.

"I'm still hungry," moaned the tiny kitten.

"My tummy feels all…thingy," Zootie complained. But her pain had nothing to do with hunger.

Soon Zootie cradled in her arms a pair of tiny chimps.

"I'm an uncle!" Easy exclaimed.

Bob stared in wonder at his twins and breathed, "Twice!"

All the animals congratulated the new mother.

The bull terrier said, "On behalf of us all, I'm sure the Chief would like to extend a special welcome. So listen up!"

Suddenly, all eyes were on Babe. The little pig was not prepared to make a speech. So he decided to sing a song instead.

"La, la, la. La, la, la." One by one, all the animals joined in. Except Thelonius.

"Shh!" the orangutan cautioned. But no one could hear him over all the woofing, meowing, and howling.

The singing was so loud that it carried to a nearby church where a duck named Ferdinand was resting from his quest. Yes, dear ones, Babe's old friend had followed him all the way to the city. And now the song led him to the Flealands Hotel.

"You look…different," Ferdinand said when he first saw Babe.

"Yeah, well, this place can really take it outta ya," Babe explained.

"Tell me about it," the duck agreed. "But, hey, I'm with my lucky pig. Snug and safe at last!"

But was he?

CRASH! A woman in a lab coat, a motorcycle cop, and several other burly brutes burst into the Flealands and started grabbing the animals.

One raider seized Ferdinand by the throat. "Hey, supper!" he laughed.

Babe rushed at the raider. But he easily caught the pig and cried, "Yo, breakfast!"

Then the bull terrier charged! Babe and Ferdinand escaped, but the dog was muzzled and chained.

Bob was shot with a tranquilizer dart as he tried to protect Zootie and the twins.

"Please, Thelonius! Do something!" Zootie begged. But the orangutan did not know what to do.

A terrible struggle followed. The chimps and Thelonius were captured, along with most of the other animals. The cruel intruders herded the animals into a waiting van.

"This one's useless," one raider said, tossing Flealick out of the van. The scrappy little dog bit at the woman's lab coat. She kicked him away, but her hem caught in the van's door. Determined to save his friends, Flealick clung to the woman's dress—even as the van drove away!

"Flealick!" Babe called. "Let go!"

At each turn of the van, the woman's hem tore just a little more—and the crippled dog swung closer and closer to the van's back wheels. Just before the tires could crush him, the dress ripped, and Flealick went flying! The dog tumbled head-over-wheels into a deserted side street.

Babe, Tug, and Ferdinand found him lying in the gutter.

"Flealick?" Babe asked. He licked the dog's snout. "Are you okay?"

"Don't worry," Flealick said. "I got their scent. They went this-a-way."

Babe sniffed the air. "Actually, Flealick, I think it's *that* way."

Babe followed the scent of his captured friends through the city to the University Hospital complex. In a room on the top floor, they found the animals.

"It's the pinkness!" Bob cried.

"Chief! I'm proud of ya," the bull terrier barked.

"May I suggest we stay calm, maintain a tight formation, and proceed in an orderly fashion," said the little sheep-pig.

"And may he suggest we do it real fast!" Ferdinand quacked.

Meanwhile, Mrs. Hoggett was in court. Luckily for her, the judge hearing her case had never forgotten the pigs of his childhood. Perhaps it was these fond memories or maybe his own round, pink face and tiny, twinkly eyes. But whatever the reason, the judge banged his gavel and cried, "Case dismissed!"

The farmer's wife was free!

Mrs. Hoggett hurried back to the Flealands Hotel. She found Babe's footprints in dirt spilled on the floor.

The landlady was as eager to find her animals as Mrs. Hoggett was to find Babe. She loaned Mrs. Hoggett the only clothes she had that would fit her: Uncle Fugly's spare clown costume!

Soon Mrs. Hoggett and the landlady were on the trail of their beastly brood. They rode Uncle Fugly's double bicycle to the University Hospital.

There Mrs. Hoggett found a kitchen helper. "We're looking for some, er, animals. A pig. Cats. Dogs. Monkeys…that sort of thing," she said.

At that very moment, the elevator doors in the back of the hospital kitchen slid open. The astonished chef dropped an armful of pots and pans at the arrival of a pig, cats, dogs, and monkeys!

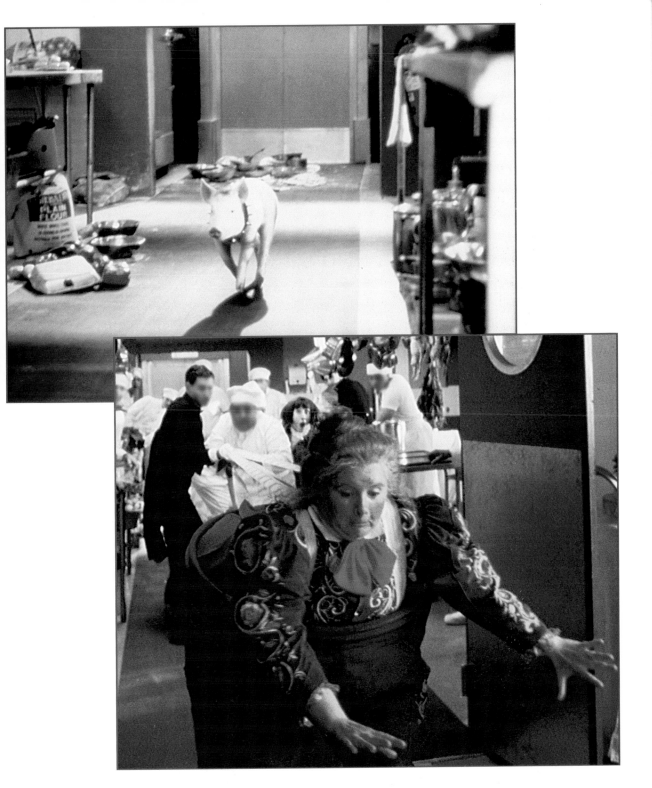

"Pig! Pig!" the farmer's wife cried.

Mrs. Hoggett reached for her Arthur's pig. But the hotheaded chef grabbed her by the clown suit's trick suspenders. The straps stretched and stretched until they could stretch no farther. With a loud *THWACK!* Mrs. Hoggett shot backward.

Babe stared after her. "Ferdie, the Boss's wife…she's here!"

To Thelonius, the figure in the clown suit looked like his beloved Uncle Fugly. "Himself," the orangutan breathed. "I thought I saw Himself."

But there was no time for tender reunions. The frantic chase went from the kitchen to the nearby ballroom, where a fancy charity banquet was in progress.

Mrs. Hoggett tried to hold off the chef and the waiters with a fire extinguisher. But she soon found herself cornered on a balcony. Her only chance was to swing to the other side. She grabbed one of the golden drapes that hung from the ceiling. She swung across the room, then tied the drape to her trick suspenders. "I'm Esme Cordelia Hoggett! And I've come for my Arthur's pig!" she cried.

Then she bungee-jumped off the balcony and bounced toward the chef who had grabbed Babe. But Mrs. Hoggett only managed to capture the chef's hat.

On her next swing, she landed on a food trolley and rode it right into the chef! Babe was thrown free and landed in a mountain of creamy cakes.

The chef grabbed on to Mrs. Hoggett's feet and started swinging her by her trick stockings. Babe butted the chef in the knees, and the farmer's wife went flying into a waiter, who pulled the DO NOT PULL tag on the clown suit. Suddenly, the clown suit inflated and Mrs. Hoggett turned into a human balloon!

Security guards rushed into the ball-room. Waiters tried to herd Babe toward the guards. Mrs. Hoggett made another swing, but the chef had grabbed a golden drape of his own and swung right into her, throwing her off course.

Suddenly, Thelonius sprang into action! The graceful ape climbed up a column, grabbed a golden drape, and swung across the ballroom to land at Mrs. Hoggett's side. He stared at the human in the bright costume. Mrs. Hoggett gave a shy smile.

Then she looked down. The security guards had captured her pig! While Thelonius diverted the chef, Mrs. Hoggett bounced down and grabbed her Arthur's pig! Finally, Babe was safe in his human's arms!

But the chimps, who had taken shelter in the chandelier, were in big trouble. The weight of the pig, the orangutan, and the farmer's wife caused the huge fixture to fall! All the chimps escaped, except for one of the babies. He was stuck on the ceiling, clinging to a fragile fragment of plaster!

"Thelonius!" Babe cried.

The orangutan was busy helping Mrs. Hoggett to her feet.

Up on the ceiling, the baby chimp sneezed. The plaster broke!

"Look!" Babe commanded.

Thelonius looked up just in time to hold out his arms and catch the tiny chimp.

"Thank you!" cried Zootie and Bob.

Thelonius looked thoughtful, then said, "Thank the pig."

The society matron leading the banquet sighed. "Much more exciting than last year," she said, with a twinkle in her tiny, piglike eyes.

Things can't always be put back the way they were. But sometimes two broken halves can make something even better. So it was that the Flealands Hotel was rented out as a dance hall.

Hoggett's farm became a sanctuary for the landlady's animals. The city animals quickly acquired a taste for country life. The chimps took to the trees, where their babies grew up strong, healthy, and chimpish. Flealick found the pace a little slow, so he took to chasing trucks.

As for the orangutan, Thelonius insisted on staying at the farmhouse with *Herself*. The bull terrier found romance with the poodle, and together they had puppies.

And finally, dear ones, the pig and the farmer were content again in each other's company. Things were back where they had started, more or less. Arthur Hoggett finally fixed his well. And as clear water gushed from the tap, the farmer turned to his pig and said simply, "That'll do, Pig. That'll do."